The Sand Castle

BY MICHÈLE DUFRESNE

CONTENTS

Pioneer Valley Educational Press, Inc.

CHAPTER 1
The Sand

Bella and Rosie were at the beach.

"I like the beach," said Bella.

"Me, too," said Rosie. "I like the beach, too!"

"I like the sand," said Bella. "I like digging in the sand! I am making a hole."

"Wow!" said Rosie.
"Look at this!
It's a sand castle."

"Wow!" said Bella.
"It's a beautiful
sand castle!"

Bella and Rosie ran
up the beach.
They looked at the sand.
They looked at the water.

Bella and Rosie looked
at seashells.
They looked
at horseshoe crabs.

Then Bella and Rosie
went back down the beach.

"Oh, no!" said Rosie.
She looked up the beach.
She looked
down the beach.
"Where is
the sand castle?"
Rosie asked.

"The sand castle is gone!"
said Bella.
"Where is
the sand castle?"

Where was the beautiful sand castle?

CHAPTER 2

A New Sand Castle

The next day Bella said to Rosie, "Let's go to the beach!"

Rosie and Bella went to the beach. They sat under the umbrella.

"Come on," said Bella. "Let's not sit around all day. Let's play."

"I'm sad," said Rosie. "I'm sad because the sand castle is gone."

Bella ran up the beach.
She saw a big,
new sand castle.
It had a ditch that
went all around it.

Bella ran back to Rosie.

"Rosie, come and look!"
she said.

"No," said Rosie.
"I am sad. I am too sad
to play today."

"Come on!"
Bella said again.

Rosie went with Bella.

"Look!" said Bella.

"Oh, look!" said Rosie.
"A beautiful, new
sand castle!"

"I love the beach,"
said Bella.

"Me, too," said Rosie.